Chasing Wild Goose Will Not Give Golden Egg
Motivational Guide For Young Souls

Devajit Bhuyan

Ukiyoto Publishing

All global publishing rights are held by

Ukiyoto Publishing

Published in 2023

Content Copyright © Devajit Bhuyan

ISBN 9789360164348

All rights reserved.
No part of this publication may be reproduced, transmitted, or stored in a retrieval system, in any form by any means, electronic, mechanical, photocopying, recording or otherwise, without the prior permission of the publisher.

The moral rights of the author have been asserted.

This book is sold subject to the condition that it shall not by way of trade or otherwise, be lent, resold, hired out or otherwise circulated, without the publisher's prior consent, in any form of binding or cover other than that in which it is published.

www.ukiyoto.com

Dedicated to my wife late Mitali Bhuyan, Advocate and Notary of Guwahati High Court who always helped young souls

Preface

The new Millennium has new openings and opportunities for the young people. But majority of the twenty first century teens and young souls are chasing wild gees or running after mirage. While it is necessary to dream big to achieve success in life, it is equally important that our new generation young stars know what is reality and what is mirage. Instead of chasing wild gees, they should be able to see life in true perspective and work with a proper plan to achieve success in life and become a good citizen and good human. In the changed world, what ever a student may be studying: be it Arts, Commerce or Science, or they pursue a career in sports, music, fine art etc there are immense opportunities in every field. But, one must have the **right aptitude** and **right potential**. It is important that one know himself first what he likes and in the area where he has the potential, rather than what is considered prestigious and glamorous for success in life. Unfortunately most of the young people opt for a career only going through hype without doing any personality test, SWOT analysis and by the time they realize that they were chasing wild geed it is too late.

There are already many motivational books for the adult people how to succeed in life but there are very few to the young souls relevant to Indian context. CHASING WILD GEES DOES NOT GIVE GOLDEN EGGS: is specially written for the students and youth of rural India and North East India. However this book also be useful to students of the cities and urban India. Author shall be highly obliged and glad if the readers point out the shortcomings in the book to be corrected in the next edition.

Contents

Why people chase wild Gees?	1
Aim, Goal and Mission	3
Maslow's Hierarchy of Human needs	5
Carrer and Values	8
The percentage syndrome	10
Time Management	13
A Stitch In Time Saves Nine	17
Failure	21
Success	25
Benchmarking	31
SWOT Analysis	35
I have the power; I can	44
Teaching of Gita for Young Souls	47
Decide your Owm Course of Life	50
The Final Diagnosis	52
My Realization and thought at 40	54
What Education Is For?	56
How To Be A Winner And Become Successful In Your Career	59
Mritasanjivani for the young soul (adopted)	62
The Transcript Page for Action	65

About the Author   *68*

Why people chase wild Gees?

When a child is born he comes to a world protected by mother, father, family members and the society as a whole. But slowly as she/he grows up, enters the hazards of living in this complex world. The family members who once fed him, protected him, did everything for his/her pleasure, comfort not only pushes him to fend of his own and survive but also ask for a price forcing him to a journey where only the fittest can survive.

A young child need not chase wild gees nor bother for his road. In the present day nucleolus family, every thing is set, every thing is well defined by parents and spoon feeding being the order of the day when children are let free majority of them become directionless. Unlike lower order animals where survival means only food and protection against hostile natural forces like heat and cold, survival for human beings means many more.

Why we chase wild gees:

01.Lack of clear vision: The range of visibility of our necked eye is only few kilometers. And also the vision of majority of people is too short, narrow or limited. Vision means ability to view a subject, problem etc imaginatively; foresight and wisdom in planning and realistic approach to resolve the problem and find a meaningful solution. Some times vision also means far-sightedness.

02.Lack of Mission: Though we come across the word mission day in and day out very few people have a mission in their life like Mother Teresa. **Mission** *means a fight with a specific purpose. The errand or purpose for which one is sent—that for which one has been or seems to have been sent into the world.*

03.No set objective and goal (short time and long time):

04.Desire for comfort and free meal without any work:

05. Parental, peer and social pressure:

06. Desire for instant fame and glorification:

07. Alladdin syndrome i.e. too much belief in miracle, fate and destiny:

08. Not knowing what we want in life:

09. Too much importance on money as the end result:

10. Infinite capacity of mind to imagine and dream big and limited capability of body & mind to work for achieving the same:

11. Not knowing one's own strength and weakness:

12. Heard mentality and following success stories without any analysis and reason:

13. Religious, social and cultural superstition:

14. False satisfaction or pride associated with particular job/profession and career:

15. Lack of mentor, guru and guide:

16. Grass on the other side of the fence is always green forgetting that all that glitters are not gold:

17. Looking at the world through colored glass:

18. Cynical and negative attitude towards life:

19. Failure to distinguish between opportunity and hurdle as opportunity comes in the disguise of hurdle:

20. In ability to recognize the motivating force and drivers of life:

Aim, Goal and Mission

There is a misconception among most of students and young people regarding the meaning of the words "aim in life". Becoming a Doctor or Engineer may be a milestone in the long journey of life but it cannot be the sole aim of life. It is because of this false notion that many of the young people became frustrated at the age of 23 or 25. Their aim of achieving something ends on becoming a doctor or engineer as they did not have the vision beyond becoming a doctor or engineer or they never thought it is required at all in the long journey of life.

So it is very important the terms **AIM, GOAL, AND MISSION**.

Aim: Aim means to direct a course. To direct an utterance with personal or special application. To direct one's intention and endeavours with a view to attainment.

Goal: The finishing point of a race. A pillar marking the turning point in a roman chariot race. An end.

MISSION: A fight with a specific purpose. The errand or purpose for which one is sent—that for which one has been or seems to have been sent into the world.

Before you decide for a career you must know your aim, goal and mission of life. Once you are clear about your aim and goal it is easy to achieve it. A mission of life will give a purpose of better living as life is not career alone.

WHY GOAL IS IMPORTANT?

All human behavior is goal oriented. People behave the way they do because of their need to achieve certain things. These goals may deal with physiological needs, psychological needs or high order social needs.

Man is one of the idlest animal. Man like free meals, free gifts and of course, if possible Aladdin's magic lamp. Man will not work unless he is forced to work to meet some of his need. Research has shown that human beings want *things in a certain order of priority. First of all, human beings must satisfy their physiological needs like food, clothing, shelter etc. Until they have enough of these, all their activities will be directed towards obtaining them.*

Once they have their physiological needs satisfied to an optimal level, a second order of needs comes to the surface and directs their behaviors. These are safety and security needs. Human beings want to make sure that they will continue to have their physiological needs satisfied. They require job security and protection from any physical and psychological dangers.

Once they have an optimal level of security a third order needs come into operation and direct behavior of human being. These are needs for love and belongingness. Human beings want affection from fellow-beings, often a selected few, and those in their immediate environment. Community organizations, student's organizations etc satisfy this need for belongingness.

Once the need for love and belongingness are also satisfied, another set of needs which may be called "higher order social needs" comes to the surface and directs the behavior of people. These needs include the needs for achievement, recognition, status, power and influence over others. These are also called "ego needs" or "esteem needs". When these social needs are also satisfied, then come the needs for understanding one's own abilities and potentials and using them to the maximum. This need is called the "self-actualizing need".

This need hierarchy theory was first developed by Abraham Maslow and hence it is called Maslow's Need Hierarchy. Most of the people are struggling with one or more of these needs and the productivity or output of his work depends upon how much he want to achieve or fulfill these needs. If one has higher order needs, he will work more, work hard and those with lower order needs would work less.

Maslow's Hierarchy of Human needs

Though I have told that man is the idlest animal, it is also a fact that man is the most intelligent animal. Man is also a social animal. Man can't live by bread alone as we have seen in Maslaw's hierarchy of needs. All human beings strive for a healthy body and a comfortable, happy and peaceful life. It is the human mind, which can guarantee a healthy body and a happy life. The choice of vocation or occupation or **career** *as we popularly call it can make or mar this happiness. The mind, body and environment are in a state of dynamic interaction and the maintenance of this interaction in optimum state of efficiency is what health and happiness means. We should not forget the age-old saying* **"health is wealth".** *The choice of a vocation should based on whether it allows* *for a healthy physique and active mind. Greed for money has killed many a promising individual, who refuses to see the truth of this:* **"You may win in one way and lose in another. You may buy gold too dear; if you give health for it, you make a poor bargain. If you sell freedom for it, you give pearls for a bubble. If you give soul for it, your self respect, your peace, your manhood, your character, you pay everything for it".**

So, choose a vocation, which is clean, useful and honourable. Choose a vocation which is refining and elevating; a vocation you will be proud of; a vocation that will enlarge and expand your manhood/femininity and make you a better human.

Many a man "… has dwarfed his manhood, cramped his intellect, crushed his aspiration, blunted his finer sensibilities, in some mean, narrow occupation just because there was money". Prestige and honour are another two reasons why people make a wrong choice while choosing their vocation or career. Many a young man has chosen the respectable, honourable and high prestige vocation of engineering, medicine or the administrative services, for which thy have no aptitude, only to become ridiculous, later on in life (leading a frustrated, unhappy life).

Remember that starting life in the right direction where even a small step will count far more than the greatest effort in the wrong direction. You can't bring back the past or lost time to start your journey afresh. Let me quote you a story from Shiv Khera's book, 'You Can Win':

Some animals in a forest decided to start a school. The students included a bird, a squirrel, a fish, a dog, a rabbit and a mentally retarded eel. A board was formed and it was decided that flying, tree climbing, swimming, and burrowing would be part of the curriculum in order to give a broad based education. All animals were required to take all subjects.

*The bird was excellent at flying and was getting **A**s but when it came to burrowing, it kept breaking its beak and wings and started falling. Very soon, it started making **C**s in flying and of course in tree climbing and swimming it was getting **F**s. The squirrel was great at tree climbing and was getting **A**s, but was failing in swimming. The fish was the best swimmer but could not get out of the water and got **F**s in everything else. The dog didn't join the school, stopped paying taxes and kept fighting with the administration to include barking as part of the curriculum. The rabbit got As in burrowing but tree climbing was a real problem.*

It kept falling and landing on its head, suffered brain damage, and soon couldn't even burrow properly and got Cs in that too. The mentally retarded eel, who did everything half as well became the valedictorian of the class.

We should also not forget the story of the cat, fox and the dog, where the fox even after knowing hundred tricks was killed by the dog as he could not decide which trick to use, but the cat saved its life by simply knowing one thing, that is climbing of trees.

We are all gifted with some strengths *and of course with some weaknesses. We should concentrate more on developing, strengthening our strength and potential. Every individual/student should do SWOT (Strengths' Weakness, Opportunities, Threats) analysis before deciding for a career. And once you made the right choice at the right time, certainly you got walkover in the qualifying match.*

> Failure in many of the cases is nothing but wrong choice or selection. Had the captain choose to bat looking at pitch condition instead of bowling in the match, his team would have own. But his wrong choice lead to his team's failure. Use your judgement to make the best choice, when choice is in your hand. Your choice may make or break your career.

Carrer and Values

*Whenever we speak about value in present day context, one thing always come to our mind, that is **money**. This is because we measure all our worldly materials in terms of money. As long as we consider material objects or material values as the primary objectives of life, it is difficult to define value or formulate a concept of value in the true sense. Whenever there is a clash between a material objective and abstract concept of value, we normally adhere to the material objective rather than to abstract concept of value. But it is not that money alone is the measure of value. When we look at our life from a broader prospective like mission, goal and objectives then there come the concept of value.*

The concept of value is a dynamic one. The concept of value is also not an absolute one. It is a relative concept. What was value during the days of crusade and sati is not value today. What is value in France may not be value in Afghanistan. Though value or value system is not an universal one, there are some universal factors or things, on which the value or value system is based or depends.

In simple words, we can say, value is the average of the sum total of believe, geography (physical and political), ethics, economy, education, technology, need and greed, environment etc. But there are some factors in value system like **truth, honesty, courtesy, virtue, integrity, justice, commitment, love etc** *which are universal and eternal.*

We as a society and human being are loyal to value system. This is because unlike lower order animals, we can't live with bread alone. If we don't have a scientific and rational value system, we can't have a harmonious, peaceful and better society to live in. However as the concept of value is an abstract one, we can't have a unit like money (rupees, pound or US$). Being an abstract concept in the whole, sometimes we as a human being or society are irrational in determining value of even materialistic things. We give more values to gold and diamond, which had little use than iron and aluminum. So certainly there may be some ambiguity in abstract concept of value, but this does not mean that money alone is measure of *value.* A society becomes good or bad, based on the values of individuals and society as a whole. And what gives society its strength is its value system. Any society that has lost its moral bearing is heading for disaster, because all failures in history were moral failures. During recent years technology has changed the value or value system most in comparison to other factors. In the digital world of Information Technology and computers, the new generation is better equipped to know things/information or acquire knowledge simply by click of a mouse. But in the absence of any well-defined value system, they think that whatever they see on the TV or computer screen are of values and what they did not see are of no values. They think car, mobile, sex, beauty queen and money are only thing of values. But this lead to broken homes, unfulfilled life, depression, guilt and an unruly chaos society. In a society where relationships are determined by how much money is in your pocket, it would be futile to speak about values.

While choosing a career one must give due importance to values he/she respects. Over emphasis on money will lead to collapse of mental peace, happiness and family life, and then money will be a useless piece of paper without any significance.

The percentage syndrome

My friend Rajiv did not attend office for three days without any information, I thought he might fall sick and so I went to his residence to inquire about his health. When I reached his home, there was an unnatural calm in his residence which I other wise never observed. I pressed the bell and Rajiv opened the door with a dim smile. What happened to the man who was always cheerful and energetic. "Are you O.K.? Is your family O.K.?" I asked him. He replied that he is O.K. but all not well with the family. When I inquired what is the matter, he replied that his son could not do well in the higher secondary examination and could manage only 50% marks. As every body in the family had high expectation, now whole family could not recover from the shock and he also see darkness ahead for his only son. I tried to console Rajiv, his wife Neeta and his son. But it was a difficult task.

Coming back home, when I opened the newspaper, I got a news item where it was written that one young boy and two young girls committed suicide due to poor performance in the higher secondary examination. I was very much disappointed to know that three young people lost their lives due to a system, which we have encouraged and propagated without any rational. Of late we are propagating a culture or system through which we measure a young man's potential, lifeline only on a 100-point scale. If a student or young man is 90% plus we branded him as good and if a student is 50% minus we branded him or her as bad. (Let God help those who failed in the examination). We don't consider other factors at all or we simply forget all those while branding a young man good or bad. Though the student with 50% minus is an honest young man with good moral character, who helps his neighbour, respect his teacher and elders, helps parents in household activities, his proficiency in art and craft all becomes irrelevant. We simply branded him as bad student. But his friend, who was unruly, intolerant, misbehaved with seniors, do eve teasing suddenly became very good. We brand him as good student, successful student and role model. Because he got 90% plus in the examination.

Is life a measure of 100-point scale? We all know it is not. Life is a much bigger domain. Life is a mission, character, integrity, sincerity, *empathy, sense of duty, commitment, love and respect for human values. Life simply can't be measured on a 100-point scale. It is nice to get 90% plus in the exam, but it does not mean that 50% minus is the end of life, end of family, end of world. I feel sorry for my friend, but he is not the only one suffering from 100-point syndrome or* **percentage syndrome**. *There are thousands such young man and families who are victim of percentage syndrome. It is the time we as a parent, we as a society start to do rating of young people on the basis of values— honesty, commitment, courtesy, dignity………, not merely on a single 100 point scale.*

As mentioned earlier, all human being are gifted with some strengths/talents and of course with some weaknesses. We should allow our children to develop and improve their natural potential and talent in a natural way, instead of a mad rush for 90% plus marks in the examination. No one in the life will ever be remembered or recognised on the basis of how much percentage or marks he/she got in his/her 10th or (10+2) examination, but on the basis of his work, contribution to society, perfection in doing something in the area of his interest. Let us not force our children to run after illusive **percentage syndrome**, *rather let us allow them to acquire knowledge for enlightenment and empowerment in their own natural way so that they can become a confident and better human being to carry the torch of civilization.*

Here is a letter by Abraham Lincoln *to the Headmaster of a school in which his son was studying. This letter is still relevant for teachers, students and parents.*

"He will have to learn. I know that all men are not just, all men are not true. But teach him also that for every scoundrel there is a hero, that for every selfish politician, there is a dedicated leader….. Teach him that for every enemy there is a friend. It will take time, I know: but teach him.. if you can..that a dollar earned is of far more value than five found… Teach him to learn to lose… and also to enjoy winning. Steer him away from envy, if you can, teach him the secret of quite laugher. Let him learn early that the bullies are the easiest to lick…. Teach him, if you can, the wonder of books… but also give him quiet time to ponder the eternal mystery of birds in the sky, bees in the sun, and flowers on a green hillside.

In school teach him it is far more honourable to fail than to cheat... Teach him to have faith in his own ideas, even if everyone tells him they are wrong. Teach him to be gentle with gentle people and tough with the tough. Try to give my son the strength not to follow the crowd when everyone is getting on the bandwagon... Teach him to listen to all men: but teach him also to filter all he hears on a screen of truth, and take only the good that comes through.

Teach him, if you can, how to laugh when he is sad... Teach him there is no shame in tears. Teach him to scoff at cynics and to be ware of too much sweetness... Teach him to sell his brawn and brain to the highest bidders, but never to put a price tag on his heart and soul. Teach him to close his ears to a howling mob... and to stand and fight if he thinks he's right.

Teach him gently, but do not cuddle him because only the test of fire makes fine steel. Let him have the courage to be impatient... let him have the patience to be brave. Teach him always to have sublime faith in himself, because then he will always have sublime faith in mankind.

This is a big order, but see what you can do... He is such a fine little fellow, my son!"

Abraham Lincoln

Time Management

"*Time and tides waits for none*"- *An old proverb* .

"*In the realm of time there is no aristocracy of wealth, and no aristocracy of intellect. Genius is never rewarded even an extra hour a day. And there is no punishment. Waste your infinitely precious commodity as much as you will, and the supply will never be withheld from you ...*" **Arnold Bennett.**

One of the common problem most of the students have is that, they did not got enough time to prepare for the exam and so they could not do well in the examination. They did not have enough time to play football, play cricket, read novel, go to attend a public meeting in time, go for a movie or drop his/her mother in the beauty parlour and pickup after two hours.

But fact is that time is not really the problem. After all we all get 24 hours a day, 60 minutes in a hour, 60 seconds in a minute. No body is getting one second less or one second more. Whether it is me, you, Atal Bihari Bajpai, Bill Clinton, Bill Gates or the teens gossiping in the street corners , every body is having only 24 hours in a day. Scientist like Einstein , Newton or leaders like Mahatma Gandhi, Jawaharlal Nehru or modern day genius Bill Gates were also not lucky to have more than 24 hours in a day. So the problem was, problem is, problem will not be the availability of time but management and proper utilization of time. Most of the people never thought how to plan and do proper utilization of time. Our school curriculum never taught students about time management and very few parents sit with their children and teach them how to manage time and do better utilization of the most invaluable resource.

In advanced countries like USA, Japan, Canada, UK etc, time management is now a days has become a big business. There are hundreds of books in the market on time management. But one will find very little regarding his own time management by going through all those books spending time and money. Student or any person who is interested to utilize his time best way has to *prepare his time management schedule himself. Time management schedule for one student must be by himself, for himself and of himself. No body can prepare a best time management schedule for another person, not even by father, mother or a time management consultant. It is one who himself can make the best schedule of his time management.*

The first step to prepare time management schedule by a student or young man is to prepare a balance sheet of how he had spent the yesterday, last 24 hours or last seven days in the week. While preparing the balance sheet of his last 24 hours, one will find that he can easily divide all his activities during last 24 hours as High Priority(HP), Medium Priority(MP), and Low Priority(LP). High priorities are those things like sleeping, eating, attending class which one must do, medium priorities are those things which we should do but could postpone for the time being without any loss or consequence. Medium priorities are those things like repairing the bicycle, repairing of the electric iron, buying a text book from the market or returning a book borrowed from the library. Low priorities are those things which we can postpone indefinitely or we can even forget it. Low priorities things are like going to see a movie in movie hall or enjoying a cricket match or serial in the TV. If one can push aside the same low priority job or item day after day, week after week, at some point of time one can decide whether these jobs can be totally abandoned.

Once a person or student is able to prepare the list of priorities, he can go ahead with the preparation of his daily, weekly and monthly time table or time management schedule. It is a well known fact that majority of the students don't prepare their daily routine, weekly priority tasks and Term Planning Calendar/ Monthly calendar. A student who wish to best utilize his time and do good academic result without reducing his fun , play and other activities time must have a daily routine and preferably it should be hanged in front of his study table. While preparing a daily routine a student must be honest and sincere. If a student feels that he is weak in mathematics and strong in English, he should give more time in mathematics, not in English even though he get more pleasure reading English(till he is in the college and abandon mathematics if he opt for arts). The daily routine prepared should not be a rigid one but a flexible one and should be reviewed every month and revise it depending upon the requirement , changed scenario and experience gained.

Once a student have a daily routine, the next step is to prepare the weekly priority tasks. As mentioned earlier a student has to mark the tasks as high priority(HP), medium priority(MP) and low priority(LP) in the weekly tasks schedule. While preparing weekly task schedule you will find that some times attending uncle's marriage or a friend's birth day will be your HP task and for giving time there you have to slightly readjust your daily routine temporarily so that you don't score poorly in your half yearly examination. You may think that you can put uncle's marriage or friend's birthday on LP task and avoid these if you can't prepare well for the examination. But my opinion is that don't do that. After all life is not the combination of examinations and how much marks one obtain in the examination. Examinations will come every year but your only uncle's marriage will not come every year. Twenty or twenty five years from now nobody including you will remember or care what you score in a particular test or paper, no matter how life threatening or tense you feel for the test while appearing it. So there is and there should be always time to attend a marriage, birth day and at the same time appear in the examination and score A+. The only thing required is that one has to plan his time properly and cut low priority task if necessary and he will find that every thing is fine. At the same time one must be ready to say no when he finds that he cannot afford to go for a picnic before his examination or due to urgency in the home, even though some of his best friend may got disappointed. The simple act of saying no where necessary will help to save lot of valuable time.

Once a student has his daily routine and weekly priority tasks, he can easily go ahead preparing Term Planning Calendar or Monthly Planning Calendar. Prepare the term planning calendar showing the dates for assignments and papers to be submitted, dates of class tests/unit tests and important non-academic activities and events. After you prepare your daily routine, weekly priority tasks and term planning calendar you will find that you don't have dearth of time. You will have enough time to study, play, enjoy movie and cricket match and most important of all you will be able to achieve your goal of securing 95% plus marks in the final examination.

The important thing is that, you must be honest and realistic while preparing your plan or schedule. You can lie your mother, your teacher, but you can't lie yourself. Give more times to those things that require more effort not to the things that come easier to you. Whenever possible, schedule pleasurable activities after study time, not before. Give break for 4-5 minutes after every hour of study to refresh your mind. Be flexible to accommodate the changes and adjust your schedule accordingly.

> "In life, I have never felt the scarcity or paucity of one thing, that is time. Because my account is always became full automatically. I had faced shortages of dress, shoes, household goods, money and even water, but not time. Whenever I look at time, my wallet is always full, only my requirement of things to be purchased (I mean priority of job) changes. Some times I spend more on buying sleep, sometimes on enjoying a cricket match and some times racing like a horse to reach a target. The choice was always mine. When we tell about a man that his time is over, we mean he is no more in this world. The moment we think that I have no time, it is the end of our life."
>
> *Devajit Bhuyan*

A Stitch In Time Saves Nine

Every year with the end of December and entering of January, the examination fever runs high and having a stiff target of 95% plus marks and incomplete revisions, sleeping less seems to be the only option for most of the students. But, does sleeping less and burning more candle gives better result? The answer is certainly not. The loss of sleep results in fatigue and impairs the normal judgement of a man. Over work, anxiety, tension and fear of examination results in loss of concentration and memory also take a nosedive. As a result many students drop out from the race before it start. With anxiety running high and exam coming closer, it is foolish to think that less sleep will give better harvest. Instead, when you think that you have over worked and are loosing concentration, it is the time to switch off the lights and have a sweet dream.

What to do and how to cope up during the hopeless winter months, when most of the people like to spend their time under the blanket? The answer is don't worry, take it easy. The following tips may be helpful to keep the examination blue out and face it coolly and yet doing well in the examination:

(1) Stick to regular hours. It is best to live by one's biological clock. Sleep at the regular hours. Frequent late nights upset your biological clock and it is rather difficult to fix it back.

(2) Sleep your full quota. Never think that loss sleep would suffice—it never does. My mentor taught me that if we loose one night's sleep, it takes four weeks to reset our biological clock. Sleep the regular seven/eight hours. This will recharge your body and mind; also it will increase your productivity/efficiency.

(3) Don't compare your sleeping hours with Tom, Dick and Harry. They are different people, you are different people.

(4) Never try stimulants. Don't even succumb to the temptation of using drugs that promise to keep you awake and alert without the need of a break. Never forget that you are a human being

Tension and anxiety to perform better, not only to fulfill one's own expectations but also to fulfill the expectations of parents is a major cause that many students perform poorly in the examination or even stumped before the match (exam) actually starts (match fixing?). The cause of frustration in most of the cases is the gap between expectations and achievements. There is also an anxiety to perform better than the last examination and also perform better than rest of the class friends/relatives/family friends. The parents are also to be blamed as they compare the performance of their child with that of other siblings. It increases stress and made exams a 'do or die' situation.

In such a hopeless situation, it is very difficult for a student to concentrate in his studies and perform better in the examination. The need of the hour when students are preparing for their final exam is that they should keep their anxiety, tension low; work systematically with a plan; appear coolly in the examination like any other examination they have faced in the life and then forget it. Too much postmortem after the examination also lead to never ending tension even though the exams are over and became a thing of past.

The following tips may be helpful to students during the examination weather to keep their tension low and perform better in the exam:

01. Keep your expectations at a moderate level. It is always good to aim higher, but don't try to achieve something which is beyond the reach of your physical and mental capabilities. If you keep a realistic target and achieve it, you will enjoy when results are out, but if you dream a target, which is impossible for you to achieve, you will be a frustrated, disappointed man after the exam.

02. Don't compare your preparation for exam with your friends. They will mislead you to increase your tension.

03. The best way to ward off anxiety and exam blues is to take examination easily. After all exams are not the be all and end all of life. Life will continue irrespective of how you perform in the exam.

04. If you are of religious minded, you can pray every morning before starting your studies. If morning is not convenient to you and you are a late riser, you can pray in the evening before starting your studies.

05. Always think positive. Think that you can also win. Never think that you are not going to do well in the examination.

While continuing your studies for longer hours, if you think that you need a break, Have A Break (of course I am not recommending to have a Kit Kat).

Restart again when you feel fresh.

As exam approaches near, most of the students feel that they are running out of time. Is the clock runs faster during exam days or you are running slow? The fact is that the clock runs at the same speed as usual, in fact you run faster during exam days. But even than why there is dearth of time?

Most of the students face shortage of time when exam is only a few weeks away. This is because they did not utilised their time properly and that they did not have a time management scheme. It is better for students to prepare their time management scheme at the beginning of the session. However if a student did not prepare his time management scheme and study plan at the beginning of the session, he must have it at least 3/ 4 months before the exam starts.

The most disadvantage thing about time is that though it is free, continuous (not like municipality water taps), yet you can neither store it nor bring back the time you have lost. You can rebuild your damaged house, you can recover your lost money, you can regain your health, but you can't bring back the time which had became past. So unless you plan well in advance and best utilise your time, when exam is very near, certainly you will find that there is acute shortage of time. However, then it will be too late and you can do nothing to bring back the lost time or stop the clock of time. And like an one-day cricket match, to reach a stiff target, you will try to run faster resulting in losing your wicket. The result is declared well in advance, you are stumped before the match (exam) is actually over.

The following tips may be helpful to students during the tense, anxious and terrible days of exam fever:

01. Segregate your daily activities as low priority, medium priority and high(top) priority. Complete the high priority jobs first and then proceed to medium priority. Discard the low priority jobs/ activities till exam is over.

02. Prepare your lesson plan considering your strength/ weakness and time available with you. Finish the difficult lessons/ subjects first and left the easier one for the period before the exam, so that you can complete them in a relaxed way without any anxiety and tension.

03. Reduce your TV viewing. If possible limit it only to daily news. Instead you can listen light refreshing music (some times) while doing maths or studying lighter subjects.

04. Please say your friend NO, when he came to your home to request you accompany him for enjoying the movie Lagan. You can enjoy it in a relaxed mood once the exam is over.

05. Once you prepare your plan for the exam, stick to it with minor adjustment till exam is over. Frequent changing may lead you nowhere.

06. Once you complete your target of study positively today, you will find no dearth of time tomorrow.

And before exam starts, you will find that you have reached the target(completing studies) ahead of

time.

Do you know, a Swiss knife is 100 times costly than an ordinary knife we normally use? Is it made of Gold? No! it is also made of the same steel with which our ordinary knives are made. Then why it has such a high premium? The reason is that the Swiss knife has a sharp cutting edge 100 times better than the ordinary knife. And it all makes the difference. Every human being are made of the same materials, but if you develop and acquire a better, sharp cutting edge through knowledge and skills, certainly you will have a premium not only in the job market, but also in the society.

Failure

'Failure is the pillar of success' is a very old and common proverb known to all of us. Yet very few of us remember it when we failed in some thing, some assignment or during the period of our crisis. Failure is very common and akin to human being. In fact the foundation of the human civilization, progress of society is based on the foundation of various failures of human being through which it learnt the use of fire, wheel, electricity, computer and many more things. In our own life we learnt to walk during our childhood through failures, we learnt to ride a bicycle after falling down several times and also to write our first alphabet after several failures. Failure in fact is a learning process, which if someone tries to avoid as a matter of sufferings, matter of sorrow or matter of shame is bound to face the same. I had a friend, whom one day I asked 'what according to you is the toughest job in the world?' He replied, 'riding a bicycle is the toughest job'. I was surprised, how the job that can be done by any Tom, Dick and Harry be the toughest job in the world. I asked him why he considered riding a bicycle is the toughest job. He replied that as he could not ride a bicycle, according him riding a bicycle is the toughest job in the world. Then I inquired from him why he did not tried to ride a bicycle during his childhood. He told me that he tried to ride a bicycle during his childhood. But when he was trying to ride it one day he fell down from the bicycle and broke his left hand. After that he was afraid of any more failure and so never tried to ride a bicycle. Now you must have realized why my friend thought riding a bicycle is the toughest job. It was because instead of using failure as a stepping stone for success, he got afraid of failure. And once you are afraid of failure, you can't succeed in anything, even the simplest job of riding a bicycle.

Failure is so common phenomenon in our life that we seldom realize its importance or significance. Day in, day out we saw people with high intelligence, innovative ideas, hard working failed in life. They include our friends, uncle, parent, teachers and neighbour whom we know well. Yet we never sit few minutes alone and analyze why our near and dear ones failed. This is because we were afraid of the word failure more than the actual incident of failure. It is easier for us to learn from the real life example of our friends, relatives or peers than the success story of Bill Gates, Henry Ford about whom we read in books. We know ourselves well why we performed so badly in the examination than our private tutor or counselor. So instead of trying only to learn from success stories of successful man, we should also do simple analysis of failure stories we have seen around us and then learn not to repeat the same in our own life. Home cooked food is always easy to digest than the best food of the five star hotels. So also it is easy to analyze and understand the causes of the failure of your uncles/seniors and eliminate the same from your action, from your life and become successful.

If we dig at the success stories of great man, successful man, we find that behind every success story there are several failure stories, which remain camouflaged because our focus to know about the success, not failures. But in fact we should learn equally from the failure stories of successful man, how they turned the table, how they changed the failures into success. Once we develop the habit of learning from our failures, from the failures of others, and did not repeat the same in our own life we can avoid several steps needed to reach success, we can save precious time. The difference between a successful man and a failed man is very intangible, one had taken failure as his best teacher, best guide whereas the other had taken failure as his worst enemy, a devil always to be hate. Failure and success are in fact two sides of the same coin as one side of the coin decides who won the toss and the other side who lost it.

On Failure

(1)

Failed at something? Good

Failed again? Excellent.

You are a lucky devil you know,

to be learning from the best teacher

in the whole world.

Because that's what failure really is.

A teacher.

A rung in the ladder.

A clever device to test your talent,

Your courage, your thirst for success.
And if you preserve, and push,
and hang on long enough, and grit
your teeth, and still manage to smile,
you'll bask in the sunshine.

(2)

When things go wrong as they sometimes will
When the road you're trudging seems all uphill,
When the funds are low and the debts are high,
And you want to smile, but have to sigh,
When care is pressing you down a bit,
Rest if you must, but don't quit.
Life is queer with its twists and turns,
As every one of us sometimes learns,
And many a failure turns about
When he might have own had he stuck it out.
Don't give up though pace seems slow-
You may succeed with another blow
Success is failure turned inside out—
The silver tint of the clouds of doubt,
And you never can tell just how close you are,
It may be near when it seems so far.

So stick to the fight when you are hardest hit—It's when things seem worst that you must not quit.   *AUTHOR UNKNOWN*

> Never mind failures; they are quite natural, they are the beauty of life, these failures. Never mind failures, these little back sliding; hold the ideal a thousand times, and if you fail a thousand times, make the attempt once more.

> *"What ever you decide to do in life, just be passionate about it. Don't be intimated by competition, as success is sweeter and failure less bitter when you have given everything. Passion, perseverance and possibility are key of my success"—Jon Bon Jovi*

Success

Success! A very sweet word after which every human being, young/old ; rich/poor; beautiful/ugly runs like the horse of a race course. This is because in general success brings fame, prosperity, wealth, recognition and most of the people think that success also brings happiness. However not to speak of the young stars, many of the adults did not have any rational thinking or idea about success, after which they are running.

What is success? Like happiness success is also a state of mind. Success is a matter of attitude. Success is a matter, what you think you are capable of doing and achieving. It is a matter of perfection, matter of self-actualization. It is also a matter of recognition by society, people and leaving one's footprint on the sand of time.

Success has no standard or specific definition. Every person has his own definition of success in tandem with his goals, mission in life. For some one, earning millions of dollars and seeing its up down in the stock market is the success, whereas for some one earning a gold medal in the Olympic or World Meet is the success. For some one having a Ph.D. degree is the success, for some one climbing the Everest is the success, whereas for some one constructing a three stories building in the posh area of the city is the success. For some students getting 95% marks in the CBSE examination is the success, whereas for some students it is not success but getting good rank in the IIT JEE is the success. So it is very difficult to define 'success' in absolute terms.

One of our great grandfather was considered to be the most success full man of his time and in our family history. This was because he had four wives, more than sixteen sons, four daughters, five elephants, a large herd of cow and several hundred acres of land. But now if I want to be as successful as my great grandfather, the first thing will be that my advocate wife will divorce me and prosecute me to put behind the bar, my company will throw me out of job for polygamy, Maneka Gandhi and her 'People for Animals' will prosecute me for keeping five elephants, and ultimately I have to languish in the jail. This means that success is a relative thing, which varies from time to time and society to society. In other words, success to an individual is always not absolute but barred by two domains called time and society. Though success is a state of mind, matter of attitude, it is not absolute only from the point of view of an individual who thinks himself to be successful. A mad or psychic man may think that he is the most successful man in the world, but certainly it is not correct though it is his state of mind or attitude. To be successful, in addition to state of mind/attitude the essence of time, acceptance of society, nation, world(depending upon the level of success) in a progressive order is a must. Some people may be considered successful in village level, some may be in the district level, some may be in the state level, some may be in the national level and some may be in the world level. This means that success has no upper limit. When you are climbing the ladder of success, you can only go up, up and up... and you will realize that there are many more steps to climb, there are many more things to achieve. The unique and good thing about success is that it is boundary less like the universe, limit less like the sky and also not bounded by parameters like money, wealth, beauty, brain, physical strength, power, popularity etc etc or to any specific field, area of work or profession. That is why Lata Mangeshkar is successful singing songs, Sachin Tendulkar is successful playing cricket, Mother Teresa is successful serving the poor, M.F. Hussein is successful through painting and Jakir Hussein is successful playing tabla. That is one can become successful in any field, area or profession provided he has the passion to give his best performance and did not quit half way.

Money, wealth, power or popularity alone can never be success. Will you consider Adolph Hitler, Harshad Mehta, Nathuram Godse or Osama Bin Laden as successful man? Do our society, do our time consider them successful? Now let me ask you few simple questions.

Who according to you is the poorest (in terms of money/wealth) person among the following people:

(a)   Rajiv Gandhi
(b)   Harshad Mehta
(c)   Mahatma Gandhi
(d)   Azaharuddin
(e)   Bangaru Lakshman

Now tell, who among those persons was/is the most successful man. Let me ask another question:

Who among the following persons is the least beautiful (or not beautiful at all):

(a)   *Albert Einstein*

(b)   *Aishwarya Rai*

(c)   *Kabir Bedi*

(d)   *Ajoy Jajeda*

(e)   *Salman Khan*

Now tell who among the above people is most successful in world standard. By your own answers, you must have realized that money, wealth, beauty or physical strength are not as much important for success as we normally consider.

It is true that the question of success is a personal one, but it is judged and shaped by society, environment and time. The concept of success always goes through metamorphosis along with time. During the time of 'Mahabharata', Arjun, Karna, Dronacharya, who were expert in archery warfare were considered to be the most successful man (now you need to be A.P.J. Abdul Kalam to develop India's missile technology and nuclear bomb). During medieval age who were expert warrior with swords and can lead armies to fight a battle or crusade were considered to be the successful man. In the 1940's we have Einstein as the most successful man and in the 1990's we have Bill Gates as our role model. Of course in every time there were lot of successful people in different fields. Some times you may not be considered successful by society for a particular reason, but if your success is universal like Galileo one day you will shine.

Let us keep aside the most successful people of the world or legends of different times. Let us think about common man like Tom, Dick and Harry (and of course me). For a common man, success is always not to reach the top of the world or breaking world records like Bubka. For a common man like you and me, success means achieving some fundamental requirement of life in optimum level, in a judicious mix and then contribute some thing positive for the people, for the society, for our future generation. For a common man like us success also means reaching the sage of self-actualization of the Meslaws' need hierarchy. In life it is not possible for every individual to reach the top of the world, to be successful like Bill Gates or Michel Jackson, but if one can achieve or acquire the following ten basic things in life, and can listen the inner voice of his body and soul, and derive self-satisfaction, certainly he is a successful man.

Ten building blocks of success for common man like me and you:

(1) Education(Qualification/ Degree, knowledge, skill & wisdom)

(2) Character & Values(Moral, Ethical, Social & Human)

(3) Freedom & Independence

(4) Hard Work

(5) Health & Look

(6) Money

(7) Social Status/ Social Recognition(Contribution to society)

(8) Love, respect and belongingness(In family and society)

(9) Friendship and Popularity(Among peers and other groups)

(10) Fun, parties, disco, night club......(No man is a computer nor life is a web site)

As a young star if you can acquire the above things/ qualities in life, certainly you will be a successful man, irrespective of the profession/ career you choose to earn your bread and butter.

Success is also having one's own identity in the society, world. When a child is born, he did not have any identity. He was identified as son/daughter of somebody. Later on he gets his name, yet he is better known as son of so and so, if his parents were well know person in the society. Slowly as he rises the ladder of success, people started to identify him by his own name and as he goes up, his parents, his brothers, sisters were identified by his name. Slowly the identities of his parents were suppressed and his identity became prime for the family. Consider a person, who all throughout his life was identified by his father's name and during his death also people told that son of so and so had died. Will you consider such a person as successful? So to be successful in life, you must build your own identity even though you may be the son/daughter of successful parents. While writing about Indira Gandhi, we never need to write Indira Gandhi, daughter of Jawaharlal Nehru. Her own name alone is enough.

'All well if end is well' is a very old popular saying. The same is also applicable in the matter of success. So to be successful, it is equally important how people *think of you or write your obituary when you are leaving this world forever. According to Hindu religion and philosophy, life did not end at death, it continues beyond death. Whether you are successful man or ordinary man, one thing is fact that, you can't see or go through your obituary. But fact is that your obituary is the ultimate test of your success of failure. Though you can't see your obituary, in fact it is you, who would be going to write your obituary through your deeds, work, success or failure. After your death, your obituary may be like any one of the following:*

(1) Nobody may bother to write your obituary like any Tom, Dick or Harry as there is nothing to write.

(2) Your obituary may be like the obituary of Mr.Money Kumar Das: 'Mr. Money Kumar Das, a corrupt and wealthy engineer of Guwahati died of heart attack at the age of 60. He built a palatial house in the posh area of the city and purchased several luxury cars for his use. He consumed 6000 KG rice, 90,000 liter water, 4000 KG chicken, 5000 liter whiskey and a huge quantity of vegetables and other food staff during his life time. He left a good bank balance for his son, who is a known goon of the city'.

(3) Your obituary may be like the obituary of Mr.People Kumar Das: 'Mr. People Kumar Das, an Engineer by profession and a social activist died at the age of 50 due to heart attack. He was a lovable person and wrote 3 novels, 7 poetry books and also some thought provoking articles in the local newspapers. He was associated with many socio-cultural organizations of Guwahati and contributed lot for upliftment of people and society. He also took leading part in people's movement and was the prime mover behind the construction of the Cultural Complex at Guwahati. He lead an honest life and left behind his wife and only son. People from all walk of like expressed deep sorrow at his sudden demise.'

(4) Your obituary may be like that of Hitler or Osama Bin Laden or Nathuram Godse, whom people and society hate.

(5) Your obituary may be like the obituary of Mother Teresa, Indira Gandhi covering the full front page of all the newspapers and also coming as breaking news in BBC/CNN, world will mourn your death.

It is you who will decide and build materials for your obituary and certainly **your obituary will tell how much successful actually you were.**

> ***A short course for success:***
>
> *01. Set your goal, mission, priorities.*
> *02. Work hard. Try your best.*
> *03. Do not imitate others. Listen to your inner voice.*
> *04. Do not try to better Tom, Dick and Harry. Do your own best.*
> *05. Always tell yourself 'I am my boss and I can do it, I can win'*

Benchmarking

'*Beavers build houses; but they build them in nowise differently or better now than they did 5000 years ago. Ants and honeybees provide food for winter; but just in the same way they did when Solomon referred to them as pattern for prudence. Man is not the only animal who labors, but he is the only one who improves his workmanship*". **Abraham Lincoln**

Benchmarking is one of the leading management tools used for improvement to gain competitive advantage. It all started in 1970 at Xerox Corporation, U.S.A. In the 1960's and 1970's Xerox was the leading player in photocopying machines and the word Xerox became synonymous for photocopying. In late 1970's Japanese manufacturers started distributing their photocopiers in US at prices lower than the manufacturing cost at Xerox, USA. The first reaction was disbelief. Fuji Xerox, Japanese subsidiary of Xerox confirmed that manufacturing costs at Japan are actually lower. This set a series of actions in Xerox, which led to the concept of benchmarking. Benchmarking can be defined as "Finding and Implementing Best Practices". Benchmarking is identifying the best performer in a particular process or activity and identifying the best practices used by them to achieve the best performance. The best practices thus identified are adapted to suit the culture and environment to gain maximum benefits. In simple terms, it is learning from others rather than reinventing the wheel.

Though Benchmarking is considered to be a new management technique, in fact it is a very ancient tool known since time immemorial and nowadays used in modern management technique to improve/measure efficiency, productivity and performance of organizations as well as of individuals. In the Epic 'Ramayana' we have the example of a very tough 'Bench Mark' fixed by the King Janak for the Prince, who wish to marry his only daughter Sita. King Janak declared that he would gave his daughter's hand only to that Prince or King who could lift and break his majestic bow known as 'Hara Dhanush'. He knew it well that the most powerful Prince or King of the world could only be able to lift his bow, not to speak of breaking it. He wanted his daughter to be got married with the most *powerful hero of the world and so his Benchmark was very tough to have the right choice without fail. The rest of the story is known to all of us. Similarly in the Epic 'Mahabharata', King Drupad also fixed a very tough 'Benchmark' to choose the groom for his beautiful daughter 'Drupadi'. One has to hit the eye of a fish fixed on a rotating wheel above ground, looking at its image on a water pot on the ground. King 'Drupad' wanted to get 'Arjuna', the most expert archer of that time as his son-in-law as he wanted to settle some old score with his friend 'Drunacharya' who was also an expert archer of that time. King 'Drupad' knew it well that except 'Arjuana' and 'Karna', no warrior in the world could make it. From these stories it is clear that, benchmarking was used by man since the age of 'Ramayana' and 'Mahabharata' to determine and exploit the infinite capabilities, potential of man.*

In the auction market, we have seen that for any materials to be auctioned, there is a reserve price and unless people offer prices above reserve price, the material is not sold by way of auction. This is quite natural if we look from our day to day knowledge of business management. Now let us look at our present day examination system, where there are broad 'benchmark' to determine the performance or capabilities of the students appearing in the examination. If you secure 30% or more marks but less than 45% of marks, you will be placed in the 3rd division/class; if you secure more than 45% marks but less than 60% of marks, you will be placed in the 2nd division/class and if you secure 60% or more marks, you will be placed in the 1st division/class. Some institutions or examinations may give grade as A/B/C/D instead of marks as stated above. Of course in any examination, you have the ultimate benchmark theoretically possible to achieve, i.e. securing 100% marks.

It is very important and positive point to note that all the things told about 'Benchmarking' were already known to most of us, most of the students as it is a part of our education system, it is a part of our day to day life. Yet very seldom we use 'Benchmarking' to improve our performance, improve our efficiency. But in a competitive world, to perform better, to improve earlier achievements, you should learn to use the technique of benchmarking. The benchmark fixed by universities/institutions to judge your academic performance is too general or too broader. This benchmark is neither related to your area of interest nor based on your capabilities, talent and potential. To achieve better, to perform better whether in examination, sports, music or in life, you should fix your own benchmark. You have seen that in the field of sports 'benchmark' (or as we call it National/World/Olympic records etc) fixed by peers/seniors are the targets which new generation athletes/ sports man tries to cross or overcome and fix new benchmark for the future generation. Unless one can come very very close or near to earlier records or perform better, one participating in World Meet or Olympic knew it well that he/she is unlikely to win a medal. Because every year in the field of sports old records became history and new records were registered as 'benchmark' for new generation. You should not forget about Pole Vaulter Bubka who was famous for breaking records(or benchmark) and fix new records. Some times several records remain for years but one fine morning a young man like you breaks it to set new benchmark.

Now from the world of sports let us again go back to your academic life, real life. In your real life, in your academic life, it is you who knew your potential, talent and capabilities better than anybody else in the whole world. It is neither your parents, nor your teacher, nor your counselor who knows you better than yourself. So it is you, who can fix realistic benchmark for you. Let us take an example: During last three years examination, you have secured 75% marks. So according to you there is scope for doing better. You can fix a benchmark of 80% for you which you think is quite achievable with more work and dedication. But if you fix your benchmark at 95% seeing the performance of your friend, it is very likely that you may become disappointed for unable to achieve your benchmark. Fixing arbitrary benchmark is not only unachievable, but also leads to disaster. I have a real life experience how arbitrarily fixed benchmark may lead to disaster. Once I had to travel from Guwahati to Nowgong in Assam. The distance between Guwahati to Nowgong is normally covered in three hours by the buses. Our driver was going very slowly as there were few passengers in the bus and he hoped of getting some roadside passengers. After one hour of journey another bus overtook our bus and realizing his mistake our driver increased his speed and over took the other bus. In the meantime the third bus going ahead of these two buses realizing that two more buses are coming near increased his speed. For the next half an hour all the three buses behaving as if they were taking part in a car race. Then suddenly we hard a loud sound. The bus going just few meters ahead of us made a head on collision with a truck. The driver and five passengers died on the spot. We were thankful to god that this could have been our bus instead of the other. All these happened because the drivers of the three buses fixed arbitrary benchmark looking at the other without considering road condition or his driving capability. The arbitrary fixing of benchmark may lead to the disaster. You must be careful in every time you fix a benchmark, so that it is realistic, achievable by you with more effort and work and not lead to breaking of *your toes. One more thing you should be clear and not confuse is the difference between benchmark and goal. Goal is of broader perspective with wider domain as explained earlier, whereas benchmark is for a specific task, job or purpose.*

> **This life is a great chance. Seek for the highest, aim at that highest, and you shall reach the highest.**
>
> *Swami Vivekananda*

> *Bharat Ratna Sir M.Visvesveraya, the doyen of Indian Engineers, believed that character building and dam building were similar activities. Build your character along with youe*

SWOT Analysis

*L*ife is a never ending process of one conflict after another. Conflict is a theme that has occupied the thinking of man more than any other with the exception of God and Love. In the matter of selecting a career for life, certainly conflict will come into surface. In the mist of conflicting views by parents, teachers, peers and even within an individual, the right decision can only be taken by doing a SWOT analysis.

SWOT analysis is a management technique applied in business decision making process. Though it is business management technique, it can be well applied to other areas or activities of human life, especially in selecting a **career**. SWOT analysis means analysis of **STRENGTHS, WEAKNESSES, OPPORTUNITIES and THREATS**. In SWOT analysis for deciding a career, strength refers to competitive advantages and other distinct competencies, which an individual can exert in a particular career/profession, weakness refers to constraints, shortcomings or obstacles which check movement/growth in certain desired direction, and may also inhibit individual in gaining a distinctive competitive advantage in his/her career/profession. A threat is a challenge posed by an unfavourable trend or development in the environment that would lead, in the absence of purposeful action, to the erosion of the individual's position or career growth. An opportunity is an attractive arena for an individual's action in which the particular individual would enjoy a competitive advantage.

An individual operates in an external environment full of opportunities and threats. From an individual's viewpoint, it is helpful to visualize the total environment comprising mega, micro and relevant environments. The analysis of individual's capabilities and weaknesses becomes a pre-requisite for successful selection of career and then success in the career and life as a whole.

Majority of the man has a tendency to follow others, to do what others are doing, instead of deciding himself what he should do based on his strengths and capabilities. We always see to our neighbours, peers what they are doing. We envy our neighbour's successful career and try to copy the same to our own life without analyzing why he was successful in his career. This is one of the reasons why most of the young people made a beeline for IT and Computer courses without giving any thought or analysis. If my neighbour had succeeded in IT career why not me?

The Elephant is one of the strongest animal. But the Elephant did not know how much strength he is having and that is why a man with a small knife can control him, but a Tiger or Lion knows his strength and so you can't control him with a knife. If you know your strength through SWOT analysis and utilize it, you are going to be like the Tiger or Lion, but if you don't analyze the conflict of your Strengths and Weakness, certainly you will be carrying loads for others like the Elephant.

As a young man, you may not be aware how to do your SWOT analysis. In order to do your SWOT analysis, complete the following self-appraisal adopted for this purpose. This self-appraisal will help you to identify your strengths and weaknesses and in deciding a career for you.

QUALITY NUMBER ONE: **POSITIVE SELF-EXPECTANCY**

<u>Synonyms</u>   : *Optimism, enthusiasm, hope*

<u>Antonyms</u>   : *Pessimism, cynicism, despair*

<u>Proverb</u>   : *"That which you fear or expect most will likely come to pass. The body manifests what the mind harbours".*

<u>Self appraisal:</u>

01. *Am I generally optimistic about all aspects of my life? How?*

02. *Do I expect the best of health(health is wealth) for myself? How?*

03. When I am discouraged, am I indulging in a form of self-pity? Illustrate.

04. *Do I look at problems as potential opportunities? Illustrate.*

05. *Do I praise or criticize more often? Describe.*

QUALITY NUMBER TWO: **POSITIVE SELF-MOTIVATION**

Synonyms : *Desire for change, excitation, urge*

Antonyms : *Fear, compulsion, inhibition*

Proverb : *"Winners dwell on their desires(rewards of success), not their limitations(penalties of Failures)".*

Self-appraisal :

01. What are my dominant fears?

02. What motivating effect do these fears have in my life?

03. What are my dominant desires?

04. Do I focus most of my attention and thoughts on these desires? How?

05. Do I focus on the rewards of success more than the penalties of failure? Illustrate.

QUALITY NUMBER THREE: POSITIVE SELF-IMAGE

Synonyms : *Constructive imagination, visualization, creativity*

Antonyms : *Dark imaginings, worries, neuroses*

Proverb : *"What you see is what you get".*

Self-appraisal :

01. Do I still hold great dreams for my future? What?

02. Do I fantasize and imagine my monthly and yearly coming attractions? Examples?

03. Is my self-image a goal-achieving mechanism or is it a self limiting handicap?

04. What are my greatest talents?

05. What am I not good at? Why?

QUALITY NUMBER FOUR: POSITIVE SELF-DIRECTION

Synonyms   : *Goal-seeking, purpose oriented, cybernetic*

Antonyms   : *Aimless, non-specific, wandering*

Proverb   : *"What you get is what you set".*

Self-appraisal   :

01. What is my most important lifetime goal?

02. What is my most important priority next month?

03. What is my objective for next year?

04. Where do I want to be five years from today?

05. What should be my position and standings at the age of 60?

QUALITY NUMBER FIVE: POSITIVE SLEF-CONTROL

Synonyms   : *Self-determination, volition, choice*

Antonyms   : *Illusions, indecision, chance*

Proverb   : *"Life is a do-it-to-myself project. I take the credit or the blame for my performance".*

Self-appraisal   :

01. Am I basically a lucky or unlucky person? How?

02. Are there a lot of 'have' than 'have not' in my life? What?

03. Are my choices in life limited or unlimited? Illustrate.

04. What are the different controlling influences in my world?

05. How can I better control what happens to me?

QUALITY NUMBER SIX: **POSITIVE SELF-DISCIPLINE**

Synonyms   : *Achievement simulation, drill, practice, regular.*

Antonyms   : *Repetitive error, inconsistency, lack of follow-through, irregular.*

Proverb : *"Habits being as harmless thoughts—like flimsy cobwebs—then, with practice, become Unbreakable cables to shackle or strengthen our lives"."Habit is the second Nature".*

Self-appraisal :

01. *Do I complete the projects I begin? Examples?*
02. *Do I have the habit of rehearsing in my imagination? Describe.*
03. *Do I have the number of bad habits that I am unable to break? Illustrate.*
04. *Do I have an excellent memory? Do I have any good habits? Illustrate.*
05. *Am I totally focussed about my success in a given field? What?*

QUALITY NUMBER SEVEN: **POSITIVE SELF-ESTEEM**

Synonyms : *Self-worth, self-respect, self-confidence*
Antonyms : *Self-deprecation, self-doubt, self-pity*
Proverb : *"If you love yourself, then, you can give love away. How can you give what you don't feel"?*

Self-appraisal :

01. *Do I accept myself just as I am today?*
02. *Is there anyone I envy or would like to change places with? Who? Why?*
03. *Am I an extremely humble person?*
04. *Do I feel guilty when I indulge myself in some selfish activity?*
05. *Is it easy for me to accept compliments and praise from others? What impact criticism have upon me?*

UALITY NUMBER EIGHT: **POSITIVE SELF-DIMENSION**

Synonyms : *Total person (Complete Man), visionary, humanist*

Antonyms : *Shallowness, egocentricity, superficiality*

Proverb : *"When you create other winners like yourself, life will pay you back and shine its sun upon your face and put the wind at your back".*

Self-appraisal :

01. Do I share my success with others freely?

02. Do I spend time generously sharing with my family and friends?

03. Do I believe in "Do unto others as I would have them do unto me?"

04. Do I spend much time living in memories of previous better times?

05. Do I spend much time dreaming about the things I'd like to do some day when the time is right?

QUALITY NUMBER NINE: *POSITIVE SELF-AWARENESS*

Synonyms : *Self-honesty, empathy, openness*

Antonyms : *Dishonesty, insensitivity, 'tunnel vision'*

Proverb : *"Oh Great Spirit, grant me the wisdom to walk in another India's moccasins for a mile before I criticize him or her".*

Self-appraisal:

01. Do I see great opportunities for improvement in my environmental, physical and mental activities?

02. Do I honestly know my own limitations in my personal, intellectual and academic life?

03. Do I try to grab opportunities in new areas or find security in already established areas/fields?

04. How would I like to cope with changes and the uncertainties in the field of career/life?

05. 'Child is the father of the man.' How would I like to be parent in future?

QUALITY NUMBER TEN: **POSITIVE SELF-PROJECTION**

<u>Synonyms</u>   : *Communicative, supportive, impressive, expression.*

<u>Antonyms</u>   : *Aloof, unfriendly, unkempt*

<u>Proverb</u>   : *"How you walk, talk, listen and look is YOU".*

<u>Self-appraisal:</u>

01. *Do I project my best self at all times?*

02. *Do I listen more than I talk?*

03. *Am I an active listener, who asks many questions and asks for examples?*

04. *When I talk, do I believe what I speak or I often try to fool others through hypocrisy?*

05. *Do I try to give my best always and people feel their best when they are in my company?*

SWOT Analysis of some successful people in their own words

01. Daler Mehndi, Pop Singer

Strengths: *Passion for singing. Have performed non-stop for nine hours at times.*

Weakness: *Moody and casual some times.*

Wisdom: *A blind faith in God's Grace.*

02. Hong Eng Hoh, Sun Microsystems

Strengths: *Inter-personal skills, situational analysis and microscopic vision for detailed insight.*

Weakness: *Desire to achieve too much too soon. Expecting others to be equally receptive.*

Wisdom: *Be focussed and work hard without an overdose of reasoning. Never be afraid of failures, escaping the situation leads you nowhere.*

03. Kiran Karnik, President NASSCOM

Strengths: *Relationship management skills, ability to apply intelligence to get maximum from the situation and practically optimistic.*

Weakness: *Introvert nature and tendency to seek perfection.*

Wisdom: *Prepare yourself to accept challenges. Choose a career that interests you, but never forget to excel if you want to be acknowledged.*

04.*Amit Govil, MD, Sapient India*

Strengths: *Focussed, motivated and goal oriented. I energize people to work in harmony.*

Weakness: *Short attention span, short tempered and an urge to trust people at first sight.*

Wisdom: *Consider your professional life as a project. Define your goals and your milestones so that you don't lose track.*

05.*Dipak Jain, Dean, Kellog Graduate School of Management, US*

Strengths: *I come from a family of committed teachers. My grandfather was a headmaster of a school in Tezpur, Assam.*

Weakness: *I am perhaps too Indian by nature.*

Wisdom: *When your shadow becomes longer than your height, remember the sun is about to set.*

06.*V.N.(Tiger) Tyagarajan, CEO, GECIS*

Strengths: *Quest for life-long learning; team building and leadership approach.*

Weakness: *Life is too short to learn all I want to.*

Wisdom: *Relish challenges that bring change; assignments that create big impact. Take risks, dream big and not be satisfied.*

07.*Sanjoy Gupta, VP&GM, Amex(India)*

Strengths: *I am pretty analytical and very perceptive. Assets are my a strong relations with people.*

Weakness: *My excessive level of modesty, which is not required always.*

Wisdom: *To possess a magical ability to keep people continuously working.*

08.*Pradeep Kar, MD, Microland Group*

Strengths: Good team player, group leader, immersed in the future, easy and fun to interact.

Weakness: Need to better manage time and priorities.

Wisdom: Think of something, be passionate about it, do it and never regret. Remember, nothing ventured nothing gained.

09. Siddhartha Basu, Quiz Master and producer of Star TV's KBC.

Strengths: Suave, articulate, razor-sharp intellect, well read and charming.

Weakness: I don't hardsell myself.

Wisdom: It's every communicators dream to be associated with a humorously popular show that entertains as well as informs.

10. Kiran Bedi, Iron Lady of India

Strengths: Dare-Devilry, professional integrity, a reformist Zeal and 'my internal sense of security'.

Weakness: Impatient, often court controversies, 'I am just a doer, leaving my actions to any interpretation'.

Wisdom: You reap as you sow: sow service and reap joy; sow hard work and reap rewards.

11. Sanjay Kapoor, CEO, Bharati Cellular Ltd.

Strengths: Easily adopt to changes, be these environment, geography, culture or just anything.

Weakness: More skewed towards work than fun. Need to improve the balance.

Wisdom: Strongly believe in 'Who moves my cheese?' Change is inevitable and we have to be prepared to savor the adventure,

12. Lajinder Bawa, Oriflamme Network Marketing

Strengths: Dynamic, approachable and responsive.

Weakness: Can not find more time in a day.

Wisdom: Hard work and positive attitude is the key to success.

13. Raj Joshi, VP, Macmillan India

Strengths: Commitment, leadership capabilities, analytical skills, positive emotions, an eye for details, hard work and patience.

Weakness: *Obsession with one mission and a tendency to push things a bit too hard.*

Wisdom: *'Be conscious of your duty and do your best with careful planning, deeds and commitment. The*

gains will follow in time.'

14. Deepak Shourie, MD, Discovery Communications India

Strengths: *I follow my instincts and let passion and creativity fuse together.*

Weakness: *I am a disciplinarian and expect the same from my teammates.*

Wisdom: *Let your passion explore something different. Be a trendsetter, not a trend-follower.*

(The SWOT analysis of a adult individual or successful person shall be certainly different from the SWOT analysis of a young soul, but going through it will help you to do your own SWOT analysis in a better perspective and wider spectrum.)

SET YOUR GOAL

"To know one's self is hard to know
Wise effort, effort vain;
But accurate self-critic are
Secure in times of strain
This much of effort bring success;
I have the power; I can
So think, then act, and reap the fruit
Of your judicious plan" **Panchatantra**

After you complete the self-appraisal to do your SWOT analysis, it is the time to set your goal and mission of life. It is important to know the career drivers that motivate you most before you decide your career and mission/goal of life.

Given below are nine career drivers. All you have to do is to mark them 1,2,3... depending upon how much importance you give to particular drivers. The most important drive according to you should be marked 1 and the least important 9. Be honest to yourself.

01.	**Material Rewards:** seeking possessions, wealth and high standard of living.	
02.	**Power/influence:** seeking to be in control of people and resources.	
03.	**Search for meaning:** Seeking to do things, which are believed valuable for their own sake.	
04.	**Expertise:** Seeking a high level of accomplishment in a specialized field.	
05.	**Creativity:** Seeking to innovate and be identified with original output.	
06.	**Affiliation:** Seeking nourishing relationship with others.	
07.	**Autonomy:** Seeking to be independent and able to make decisions for oneself.	
08.	**Security:** Seeking a solid and predictable future.	
09.	**Status:** Seeking to be recognized, admired and respected by the community at large.	

After marking the career drivers according to its importance in your life, complete the following questionnaire in brief (within 50 words) and you will have your goals ready in your hand for ready reference. This will be your benchmark for future goals/mission and update your goals along with the changes of time.

01. What is your goal you want to achieve during the current year ? What is your goal after five years?

02. What do you enjoy most in your leisure time?

03. What do you think is your strengths in your personality?

04. What are your weakness?

05. How important it is for you to win?

06. What do you worry about most? Your career/ your relation with friends and parents/ any other thing.

07. Who or what irritates you most?

08. How intelligent are you compared to most people you know?

09. If a genie could give you anything you wished, what would it be?

10. What do you want in life and what price you are ready to pay for it?

11. Write the mission statement of your life within two/ three sentences.

Teaching of Gita for Young Souls

The 'Bhagavad-Gita' is one of the best motivating and path showing scripture ever written in the history of mankind. The teachings of 'Gita' is not only relevant in the matter of spiritual crisis of human being, but also equally relevant to the young souls in the matter of selecting a career/job/vocation and stepping one's way in the right direction. Some relevant verses of the 'Gita' in the matter of selecting right job/career is reproduced for the benefit of the young souls, as it may not be practical or possible for them to read the whole 'Gita' in this point of time:

(i) No man can ever remain even for a moment without performing any action. The impulses of nature deprive him of freedom in this respect and compel him to act.(Realize if your natural impulses and your career choice co-insides for the same goal, how much better you would perform.)

(ii) One's own Dharma(duty), even though not glamorous, is better than duty alien to one's growth(para-dharmah), however well performed. For even death in doing one's duty leads to one's good, while a duty alien to one's growth is burdened with the fear of downfall.(If your natural impulses are not tuned with your vocation, you will always have the fear of failure and left behind.)

(iii) He who sees work in 'no work' and 'no work' in work, is wise among man.(This is possible only if you enjoy your work.)

(iv) Defects are natural to all works as smoke is to fire. If discharged in a dedicated and detached spirit, as an offering to the Lord who manifests as society, all blemishes are overcome.

(v) Duties which your natural tendencies have imposed upon you, but which out of delusion you refuse to do, even then you will have to perform them by compulsion of Nature.(This is why many people have to change their vocation/career midway realizing that this was not my cup of tea losing precious time.)

(vi) One's own duty, even if without excellence (i.e. inferior in the scale of worldly values), is more meritorious spiritually than the apparently well-performed duty of *another. For, no sin is incurred by one doing works ordained according to one's nature (that is, in consonance with one's own natural evolution).*

(vii) Do not abandon the duty that is natural to you, even if some imperfections are incidental to it. For there is no undertaking without some imperfections, even as there is no fire without a covering of smoke.

(viii) Perform your prescribed duties. For action is superior to inaction. If you are totally inactive, even the survival of the body would become impossible.

(ix) An ignorant man without any positive faith, who knows only to doubt, goes to ruin. For such a doubting soul, there is neither this world nor the other world beyond. There is no happiness for him.

According to 'Gita', 'Svadharma' is work (or as we say vocation/career now a days) according to one's nature. The practical way of applying the Gita's teaching in this respect today is to consider the duty (vocation/career) to which one is called, as one's 'Svadharma'. But until an ideal and efficient social system comes into vogue, it may not be possible to give every one a work for which he is suited by his character type. So realistic approach would be to choose a career which is more akin to his nature after eliminating the other possible options. Unfortunately, today most men are found seeking not a duty (vocation/career) temperamentally suitable to them, but that will bring them maximum income or money. When a duty is valued solely for the income it fetches, it ceases to be a pursuit of a 'Dharma' or a spiritual value. Receiving remuneration for services is un-avoidable for man in the modern world, but what is un-spiritual is to work only for its remuneration, forgetting that work he does is an offering to God (through services to society/people), irrespective of the remuneration he gets. Young souls should also take notice of these teachings of 'Gita' while deciding a career.

Blame none for your own faults, stand upon your own feet, and take the whole responsibility upon yourselves. Say, 'This misery that I am suffering is of my own doing, and that very thing proves that it will have to be undone by me alone'. That which I created, I can demolish; that which is created by some one else I shall never be able to destroy. Therefore, stand up, be bold, be strong. Take the whole responsibility on your own shoulders, and know that you are the creator of your own destiny. All the strength and succour you want is within yourselves. Therefore make your own future. 'Let the dead past bury dead'. The infinite future is before you, and you must always remember that each word, thought, and deed, lays up a store for you and that as the bad thoughts and bad works are ready to spring upon you like tigers, so also there is the inspiring hope that the good thoughts and good deeds are ready with the power of a hundred thousand angles to defend you always and for ever.

Decide your Own Course of Life

*O*nce you have done your *SWOT* analysis, know your career drivers and set your goal, then it is not a very difficult task to choose a career and decide your own course in life for you. You know what you want in your life, you know where you have the potential, and you know where there are opportunities for you. In addition to *SWOT* analysis, goal setting and knowing the career drivers, some of the factors you should give due importance while deciding your course of life are:

(i) **Intelligence**: Intelligence include your I.Q., Social Intelligence and Emotional Intelligence (E.Q.). Total intelligence is more important to be successful in life and career than simply having a high I.Q. There are many cases where an academically brilliant executive, considered a genius in his field, had failed miserably in his career only because he did not have enough social intelligence and emotional stability.

(ii) **Personality**: You may be a person of Introversion or Extroversion. You may be a person of Dominating personality or Submissive personality. If you are of Introvert in nature, you should not choose a career, which demand people with Extrovert nature. You may be too social or you may like loneliness to do creative work. It is you yourself, who can judge your personality best. Give due importance to your personality while deciding your career.

(iii) **Interest**: All work is hard unless you care for it and are interested in it. No amount of ability, aptitude, financial backing or any other such kind of support can be of any use if the requisite interest in the job is absent. However mind that possessing a high degree of interest towards an occupation does not guarantee success in it without considering other factors.

(iv) **Special Aptitudes**: If one is good in art, it would be really sad for him to if he takes up a career where he had to work in a machine shop. M.F. Hussain can't play better cricket than Sachin Tendulkar nor Tendulkar can sing better songs than Daler Mehndi.

(v) **Physique:** *Various jobs have various physical demands and the choice should be made after careful consideration of all the relevant facts involved in it. A man with poor health and heart problem should not take a career in the mountain brigade of the army.*

(vi) **Sex:** *Though legally, socially men and women are equal, nature had given them different physique, capabilities. So some careers are more suitable for men and some for women. So this factor should also be considered by students while choosing a career.*

(vii) **Age:** *Some careers need early entry to be successful in that career. Late entry may lead to frustration due to unfulfilled ambition and necessity of working under much younger people(in age).*

By this time I think you have realized that obtaining a degree in engineering, medicine or management is not a career or be all and end all in life. It is only the first step in the career. There are some more qualities required to be developed, if not inherent in your personality to be successful in the career. For example some careers need capability to do team work. Your performance will be determined by the performance of other team players. Some careers need your capability to manage your superiors/boss and your cordial relation with them. You can not go up in the ladder in the career of management by simply doing hard work, if you can't manage cordial relation with all the person who is above you in the hierarchy. Some people may say it buttering or some may say it managing your boss, but one thing is clear that unless you have this quality, it may be difficult for you to go to the top of the ladder. There are of course some careers or profession where talent and hard working alone are enough. So remember all these things when you take a life long decision, choosing a career.

The Final Diagnosis

Y*ou are young souls! You are full of energy, enthusiasm and dreams to make something big. You are full of spice and vinegar—that is good. You are fan of Michel Jackson, Madonna and Sachin. You know your stuff too. You are up-to-date—you know things that I never did, never will now. But yet as your senior, take my advice and try to keep it that way. Don't make the mistakes I had made. Life is too short to learn everything from one's own mistake.*

As a young boy, I had also the dream to make something big, something remarkable. But unfortunately, I never started my mission of something big, something great thinking that I was still young enough and I had enough time to do it. I completed my engineering, joined my service and got relaxed. Let me do something after my retirement of service. Slowly time passed through months, years and decades. No achievement, nothing remarkable, nothing big, doing only day to day routine jobs. Then suddenly one day Mr.Bell rang the alarm and I woke up. All this happened with a small incident on the day of my 40th birthday. My boss gave me an assignment to prepare a report few months ago which I thought was time consuming and would require lot of effort. So I always postponed it for next day. In the meantime several months passed without any progress on the report. On that day there was a meeting and in the meeting suddenly boss asked me to submit the report for discussion. I told him that I had not yet completed the report as it was time consuming and require lot of data and information. My boss was not impressed and asked me to leave the meeting and not show my face to him till I complete my report. I was ashamed in front of my friends and straight went to my room and took out the papers and started preparing the report. Within two hours the report was ready with a computer printout and I went to the venue of the meeting with my report as the meeting was still going on. My boss saw me and asked me irritatingly, 'why are you here? I told you not to show your face without completing the report.' I looked to my boss and forwarding the copy towards him told 'sir this is the report'. Without looking to the report he asked me, 'did you learnt something from the incident?' I replied 'yes sir, any thing once started certainly would be finished, but if it is not started it would never be finished.' This *was a big lesson for me on my 40th birthday. After going home when I tried to make the balance-sheet of my last forty years, I found that it was a very big zero as far as my big things, remarkable things were concerned. I had never tried to start anything big any thing great in the past except thinking. So it would never be finished in my lifetime. I prepared a soul searching for myself canceling celebration of my birthday, which I am reproducing for you.*

My only suggestion is that you should not made the same mistake I had done thinking that I had enough time to do some thing big, something great. You should take lesson from my life and start the habit of doing things today. If you really do it I am sure, you are certainly going to do something big, something great and one day you would be the legend or icon of your times.

My Realization and thought at 40

"Some people from the History who lived less than me but able to make more positive contribution than me and able to keep their footprint on the sand of time:

SL NO	NAME	AGE
01	Jesus Christ	37
02	Shakkaracharya	32
03	Swami Vivekananda	39
04	Saint Gyaneshwar	21
05	King Solomon	39
06	Alexander The Great	33
07	Samudragupta	39
08	Vikaramaditya	37
09	W.A.Mozart	35
10	Yuri Gagarin	34
11	Martin Luthar king	39
12	Sriniwas Ramanujan	33
13	Bruce Lee	33

14	Subramaniyam Bharati	39
15	Sardar Bhagat Sing	24
16	Cleopatra	39
17	Marilyn Monroe	36
18	Lady Diana	36
19	Rani Laxmi Bai	24
20	Joan of Arc	19
21	Smita Patil	30
22	Divya Bharati	18
23	Anne Frank	16
24	Florence Griffith Joyner(floJo)	38

If I want to do some thing worth or remarkable and positive I must do today, because tomorrow may not come for me."

The clock of life is wound but once

And no one has the power

To tell just when the hand will stop

At late or early hour

Now is the only time we own,

Live, love and toil with a will

Leave nothing for tomorrow

For the clock may then be still.

(Author unknown)

> **Honesty is the best policy. The real dishonesty is to lie to ourselves, deceive our own soul. True satisfaction visits us only when we feel and can tell our souls that we have been 'good' and 'honest'.**

What Education Is For?

*I*n *the materialistic world most of us believe that education is only for earning money or livelihood. But the true meaning and aim of education is much wider than earning money. As long as you think that education is only for money, you are bound to chase wild gees, nothing else. The moment you realize the true meaning of education, and acquire true education, you need not chase money, it will automatically follow. All young souls must know the true aim and mission of education to become really educated in true sense.*

01. Education is to acquire knowledge and wisdom

02. Education is to acquire skill

03. Education is to learn toleration and respect values

04. Education is to enlighten and enlarge the horizon of mind to look at life without coloured glass

05. Education is to live in optimum (dynamic equilibrium) condition with nature and society

06. Education is to develop inner potentials

07. Education is to build a character

08. Education is to develop a positive attitude

09. Education is to achieve self- actualization

10. Education is also for earning a livelihood and build a CAREER

Persistence

Nothing in the world
can take the place of persistence.
Talent will not;
nothing is more common than
unsuccessful men with talent.
Genius will not;
Unrewarded genius is almost a proverb.
Education will not;
the world is full of educated derelicts.
Persistence and determination
alone are omnipotent.
The slogan 'Press On' has solved
and always will solve
the problems of the human race.
Calvin Coolidge

Education should not be a means for earning money, but a channel to change the mental, social and economic status/condition of the people of the country and the world.

"Education is an ornament in prosperity and refuse in

A Promissory Note For 21ˢᵗ Century Students that costs nothing but pays everything:

> As the supreme animal living in this planet earth, I promise that I will protect environment, ecology, bio-diversity and other weaker animals living in this earth. As the human being, I promise that I will always uphold moral, social, ethical and human values. As the citizen of India, I promise to encourage love, peace, communal harmony and brotherhood among all the people living in this country.

> Strength is goodness, weakness is sin. The only religion that ought to be taught is the religion of fearlessness. It is fear that brings misery, fear brings death, fear breeds evil.

How To Be A Winner And Become Successful In Your Career

01. Mission, Goal & Objective:
Define mission, goal and objective of your life. First thing in life is that you should know what you want to achieve in life.

01. Knowledge and Skill:
Knowledge is power and skill is the cutting edge. Unless you develop your knowledge base and sharpen your skills, it is just impossible to achieve mission, goal and objective of your life.

03. Positive attitude:
The difference between a winner and a loser in life is very intangible one and that is attitude. If you have a positive attitude, you will be a winner and if you have a negative attitude, you are bound to fail.

04. Time Management:
Be self organised and best utilise your time. Time is the best free resource, utilisation of which will make or break your career, your present, past and future.

05. Individual Self-discipline:
Can you think of success in career, life without discipline and punctuality? Set good examples for others in punctuality, leadership, initiative, efficiency and tact with a sense of responsibility.

06. Maintain Self Control:
Exercise self-control and deliberately watch our thought process and behaviour.

07. Dignity:
Respect dignity of each individual, dignity of labour and be positive and helpful to others.

08. Communication:

In this age of ***IT*** develop effective communication. Communication should be open, horizontal & vertical.

09. Ego:

Shed off negative ego and domineering behaviour. Ego is one of the causes why many talented people failed in life.

10. Avoid Arrogance:

Shed off arrogance, whether egoistic or emotional in our behaviour. Be humble without trying to throw your weight around. It costs nothing to be humble with a smile but it pays dividend, which some times you can't measure.

11. Stress Tolerance:

Practice stress tolerance with special reference to tolerance from ambiguity, frustration and hostility.

12. Be a Good Listener:

Accept and encourage thoughts of your seniors, juniors and colleagues, being empathic and understanding.

13. Taskful:

Be taskful without being hurtful.

14. Petty Mindedness:

Avoid petty thinking and do not allow it to eat up your valuable time.

15. Team Work:

The world is not a place for solo feats. Believe and encourage team-work.

16. Interaction:

Improve interaction with friends, relatives, colleagues in work and social life. Promote mutual cooperation.

17. Suggestions:

Gracefully accept suggestions from peers, subordinates, others and also constructive criticism.

18. Inter-Personal Feed Back:

Practice inter-personal feedback to correct and rectify mistakes. Give feed-back to *others but no back-biting or leg pulling.*

19. Information Distribution:

Never encroach on and monopolise information; make information available to others.

20. Resilience:

Develop enough resilience, endurance and have patience. You should be capable to over ride upheavals that beset life—natural, financial, social & emotional. There is no short cut to success.

Most people failed not because of lack of ability or intelligence but because of lack of desire, direction, dedication and discipline.

William Jantes of Harvard University

> *The marely learned is a fool,*
> *Wise man uses action's tool;*
> *For no remembered drug can cure*
> *The sick by name alone, be sure.*
>
> **Panchatantra**

Mritasanjivani for the young soul (adapted)

*L*ife is not smooth and plain as astro-turf. Life is also not bed of roses. Up-downs, failure-success, rise-fall, joy-sorrow are all part of life. Sometime in life due to various reason you may feel disappointed, depression may stop the momentum of your life. Go through the following few lines, analyze them and try to understand/absorb its inner meaning, certainly you will feel rejuvenated.

01. The hammer shatters glass but forges steel.

02. The tests of life are to make, not break us. Trouble may demolish a man's business but build his character.

03. Two man looked through prison bars—One saw mud, the other stars.

04. Great people are just ordinary people with an extraordinary amount of determination.

05. Winner don't do different things, they do things differently.

06. Storms make oaks take deeper roots.

07. When it is dark enough, men see the stars.

08. The most vital test of a man's character is not how he behaves after success, but how he sustain defeat.

09. When you are at the rock bottom, you can't go down but only up.

10. Four things come not back—the spoken word, the sped arrow, the past life or time, and the neglected opportunity.

11. Very little is needed to make a happy life. It is all within yourself, in your way of thinking.

12. Happiness is as a butterfly, which, when pursued, is always beyond our grasp, but which, if you will sit down quietly, may align upon you.

13. It's good to have money and the things that money can buy, but it's good, too, to check up once in a while and make sure you haven't lost the things money can't buy.

14. If you want to build and maintain a positive attitude, get into the habit of living in the present and doing it now.

15. We need to compete for knowledge and wisdom, not for grades (percentage).

16. Opportunities come disguised as obstacles. That is why most people don't recognize them. Remember that the bigger the obstacle, the bigger is the opportunity.

17. To experience the satisfaction and enjoyment of success in life, a definitive goal is essential.

18. Do your best. There is no goal achieved better than that.

19. Work and more work are important in achieving goals.

20. Time is the inexplicable raw material of everything. With it, all is possible; without it nothing.

21. Self- confidence is the first requisite to great undertakings.

22. The journey of a thousand miles begins with one step.

23. Never dwell on what you have lost. If you do, you will be discouraged and defeated. Look not at what you have lost but at what you have left.

24. The man who does things makes many mistakes, but he never makes the biggest mistake of all—doing nothing.

25. Enthusiasm makes ordinary people extraordinary.

26. The great are firm, though battered, as before: Great ocean is not fouled by caving shore.

27. *No treasure equals charity, No gem compares with character.*

28. *For lost and dead and past*
    The wise have no laments
    Between the wise and fools
Is just this difference.

29. *Fear fearful things, while yet*
    No fearful thing appears;
    When danger must be met
    Strike, and forget your fears.

30. *Why wealthy, puff with pride?*
    Why poor, in gloom subside?
    Since, like a striken ball,
    Men's fortunes rise and fall.

TEN COMMANDS NOT FOR PC BUT FOR SELF:
01. *Self-assertive*
02. *Self-confident*
03. *Self-control*
04. *Self-determination*
05. *Self-discipline*
06. *Self-esteem*
07. *Self-help*
08. *Self-reliance*
09. *Self-respect*
10. *Self-starter*

The Transcript Page for Action

I have completed my pages and now it is your turn to write your transcript in this final page today for action. Unless you **complete this page today** *the reading of the book will serve no purpose as this means you have not started the habit of doing things today and you will forget whatever you read like the boring evening lecture of your class.*

The mission statement of my life is:

My short term goals are:

My long term goals are:

My choice of careers are:

    (1)

    (2)

    (3)

My choice of academic courses are:

    (1)

    (2)

    (3)

My most preferred institutions to pursue my academic course are:

    (1)

    (2)

    (3)

Chasing Wild Gees

  Does Not Give

    Golden Eggs

A Motivational Guide for Young Souls

Note:

Intelligence Quotient (I.Q.) Means the fundamental intelligence all of us possess with which we carry out our day-to-day work. Human beings possess an innately high level of intelligence compared to most of the lower forms of life. IQ primarily solves logical problems.

Emotional Quotient(E.Q): Has to do with emotions like pleasure, pain, happiness and sadness. While these are part and parcel of everyday life, once they start to interfere with day-to-day efficiency and peace of mind, they take us away from normal life and living.

Spiritual Quotient(S.Q.): Is a fine balancing act. Once we begin to understand ourselves well through proper application of our intelligence and emotions we are living our lives according to spiritual principles.

About the Author

Devajit Bhuyan

DEVAJIT BHUYAN, Engineer, Advocate, Management & Career Consultant, was born at Tezpur, Assam, India, on 1st August, 1961. He completed Bachelor of Engineering (Electrical), from Assam Engineering College and subsequently completed Diploma in Industrial Management, from International Correspondence School, Mumbai, LL.B. from Gauhati University, Diploma in Management from Indira Gandhi Open University, and Certified Energy Auditor Examination from Bureau of Energy Efficiency (BEE), New Delhi. He is also a Fellow of the Institution of Engineers (India), Life member of Administrative Staff College of India (ASCI) and Assam Sahitya Sabha. He is having 22 years' experience in Petroleum and Natural Gas Sector and 16 years in education management. He has authored 70 books published by different publishers namely, Pustak Mahal, V&S Publishers, Spectrum Publication, Vishav Publications, Sanjivan Publications, Story Mirror, Ukiyoto Publishing etc. To know more about him please visit www.devajitbhuyan.com.

www.ingramcontent.com/pod-product-compliance
Lightning Source LLC
LaVergne TN
LVHW041544070526
838199LV00046B/1825